K...t...hgn
to a **Knight**

Hilda Offen

D1077382

For Cleo

CATNIP BOOKS
Published by Catnip Publishing Ltd
14 Greville Street
London EC1N 8SB

First published 2009
1 3 5 7 9 10 8 6 4 2

A CIP catalogue record for this book is available from the
British Library.

ISBN 978 1 846470 85 1

Printed in Poland

www.catnippublishing.co.uk

Contents

Contents

Welcome, Sir Wilbert!

The King and Queen of Little Twittel-berg were hurrying through the palace. They were hurrying because the wizard was chasing them. They could hear him in the distance, moaning and muttering to himself. Every so often they caught a word that sounded like 'spectacles'.

"I wonder what he wants?" said the King. "I could really do with some peace and quiet."

They scurried down a long corridor and arrived at the head of the Great Staircase.

"Stop, Your Majesty!" cried the wizard.

The King slowed down and looked over his shoulder. Unfortunately, he failed to see the skateboard at the top of the stairs.

The next moment he was careering downwards, waving his arms and trying to keep his balance. He whizzed across the Great Hall and collided with a chair.

For a moment, a thousand stars circled his head, Then everything went black.

The King came round to find two hazy faces hovering above him.

"Are you alright, my dearest?"

It was the Queen.

The King tried to answer, but no words came. The wizard thrust his face close to his. He was speaking, too.

"Someone's stolen my magic spectacles!" he snarled. "Have you got them?"

"Certainly not!" said the King, recovering his voice. "Never mind your spectacles! Send for the doctor! I think I've broken my leg!"

It was later that day. The King lay in the Royal Bedchamber, looking pale, with a large plaster cast on his leg.

"Pom!" he whispered in a hoarse voice. "There is something I must say to you."

Prince Pom approached the bedside.

"Come closer!" said the King.

Prince Pom bent down and the King croaked, "The Royal Tournament takes place in a fortnight. I am due to fight in the jousts. You must take my place."

"Me, father?" faltered Prince Pom. "I'd rather not, if you don't mind."

"There's no 'rather not' about it, Pom," said the Queen. "You owe it to your father. After all, who was it who left the

skateboard at the top of the stairs?"

Prince Pom blushed.

"I'm sorry," he said. "But —"

"No 'buts'," croaked the
King. "It wouldn't be a
Royal Tournament
without a Royal
in it. Besides, I've
already booked
your opponent."

"Oh no!" thought
Prince Pom. Aloud
he said, "What's he
like, dear father?"

"I don't know," said the
King. "I found him in the
Yellow Pages. He's called
Sir Wilbert the Weedy."

Prince Pom cheered up.

"Sir Wilbert the Weedy?"
he thought. "That doesn't
sound too bad."

"I've invited him to stay
at the palace," said the King.
"In fact, he arrives today.
I'd like you to greet him

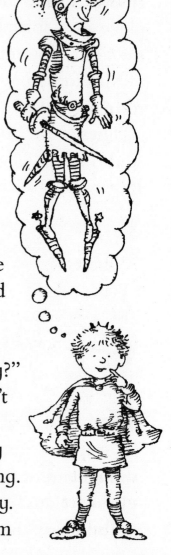

and show him to his rooms."

At that moment they heard the clatter of hooves. The Queen crossed to the window.

"He's here!" she cried. "He's early! Sir Wilbert the Weedy has arrived!"

Prince Pom made his way down to the courtyard, feeling light-hearted; he whistled a jolly tune to himself. As he stepped into the sunlight he pulled up short and stopped whistling.

A knight in a suit of shiny armour was reining in his horse. He carried a lance and a shield with a picture of an axe and a rabbit on it. A small cage swung from his saddle.

The Knight gave a roar when he saw Prince Pom and slammed up his visor.

"Hallo, Titch!" he growled. "I'm Sir Wilbert the Weedy. I've come to fight the King."

Prince Pom struggled to speak. Sir Wilbert was not weedy at all – quite the opposite, in fact.

He was enormous.

The Prince gave one of his deepest bows in order to give himself time to recover.

"There has been a change of plan, sire," he said at last, straightening up. "My father, the King, has broken his leg. I will be taking his place."

The Knight threw back his head and roared with laughter.

Ho! Ho!
Ho! Ho!

"You, Shorty-pants? You?" he gasped.
"Ha! Ha! Ha! You cannot be serious!"

The Prince showed Sir Wilbert to his
room. He watched in horror as the Knight
struggled out of his armour. Sir Wilbert
emerged like a giant pudding boiling over
from a pot.

"This stays under lock and key," said Sir Wilbert, pointing to his armour as it clanked to the floor. "I never fight without it. I said — I never fight without it!"

He touched his toes. Then he flexed his arm muscles. They were as big as cannon-balls.

"Would you like to see my mascot?" he asked.

He opened the cage and a white rabbit in a jewelled collar hopped out. Sir Wilbert grabbed it by the scruff of its neck.

"His name's Cedric," he said. "You can stroke him if you like."

Prince Pom thought it would be rude not to, so he stretched out an uncertain hand. Cedric opened his mouth and bit him.

"Ow!" said the Prince, sucking his thumb.

"Ha! Ha! Ha!" roared Sir Wilbert. "Good one, Cedric. Now, young whipper-snapper, go and ask your cook to send up a side of beef. It's been a long journey."

Prince Pom trudged off to the palace kitchens. He could hear Sir Wilbert in the distance, laughing fit to burst.

The Two-Guinea Spell

After he'd spoken to the cook, Prince Pom went off to look for Laura Jones. He found her in the town playground, hanging upside down from a climbing frame.

"Laura!" he said. "Something awful's happened. My father has broken his leg and says I must fight Sir Wilbert in the tournament."

Laura swung right round in a circle and sat upright.

"And – Laura!" wailed the Prince. "He's enormous! You should see his muscles!"

"Well," said Laura Jones. "You're much braver than you used to be, Your Highness. And I suppose you could start practising your jousting."

"It's no good!" cried Prince Pom. "I'm just no good at fighting. I can practise all I like but it won't make any difference. And you haven't seen him! Do you know what he's just said to me?"

"No, Your Highness," said Laura Jones.

"He said 'Watch out, Shorty, you're mincemeat!'" said Prince Pom. "He's really

rude. And *huge*. Why ever do you think he's called Sir Wilbert the Weedy, Laura?"

"I don't know, Your Highness," said Laura. "Perhaps it's a joke name, like 'Little John'."

"It's not a joke to me!" cried Prince Pom.

"I'm desperate! Will you come with me to see the wizard, Laura? I've had an idea."

Prince Pom hammered on the wizard's door.

"I'm not in!" came the wizard's voice.

"It is I, your Prince!" called Prince Pom.

"Clear off!" replied the wizard.

Prince Pom tried again.

"I've come to buy a spell," he called. "I've got a golden guinea."

The door opened a crack and the wizard peered out.

"It's two guineas for a spell," he said.

"Alright. Done," said Prince Pom. "Now can we come in?"

Prince Pom had never been inside the wizard's room before. He could hear Laura tut-tutting behind him; the room was in a terrible state. The tables and shelves were over-flowing with all sorts of magic equipment. There were skulls and skeletons, dried frogs, newts and glass jars full of red and green liquid. Old books spilled over the floor, along with broken test tubes, a stuffed owl and a string of fake sausages. Everything was covered in a layer of dust.

"Out with it!" said the wizard. "I've no time to waste – I've lost my magic spectacles. I left them on the windowsill and now they're gone. I've been looking everywhere."

"We could help you look for them," suggested Laura. "And perhaps we could tidy up your room at the same time?"

"No!" snarled the wizard. "I like it like it is. What is it you want?"

"I have to fight Sir Wilbert the Weedy," said Prince Pom. "He's not weedy at all – he's enormous. So I need a spell to make me strong and powerful."

"Huh!" snorted the wizard. "That's you young people all over – shortcuts to everything. Let's see the colour of your money first."

Prince Pom handed over the coins. He had been saving up for some rollerblades, but he felt that this was much more important. The wizard grabbed the money and shoved it in his pocket.

"Now – where's my spell-book?" he said and he started groping around the shelves.

"Is this it?" asked Laura.

The wizard snatched the book and thumbed through it, sticking his nose close to the page.

Laura and Prince Pom waited patiently until the wizard found the right spell.

"Aha!" he said at last. "'Spell for ex – extreme – extreme –'"

"Would you like me to read it for you?" asked Laura, but the wizard snatched the book away and snapped:

"No! My spell-book is private!"

He squinted at the page and read, "'Take one hair from a unicorn's tail – er – er – two whiskers from the Beast of Beltrane.' What's this? – oh yes! 'A thread from the centre of the Labyrinth. And – er – um! Three strands of gold from a giraffe's nest. Oh, no. A griffin's nest.'"

"Unicorns?" said Prince Pom. "Aren't they extinct? And I thought griffins were just in stories. What's the Beast of –"

The wizard interrupted him.

"Just bring me the hair from a unicorn's

tail to start with," he said.

"And then I suppose you'll pop it in your cauldron and start making a potion?" said the Prince.

"Questions, questions," growled the wizard and he opened the door and pushed them both out.

"But however do we catch a unicorn?" asked Prince Pom, backing away down the corridor.

"Put salt on its tail!" said the wizard, and with a wild cackle of laughter, he slammed the door shut.

Elfrida Wildwood

The next morning a herald brought Prince Pom a note from Laura Jones. It said "Meet me at the jousting ground. I have found a unicorn."

The Prince grabbed a salt cellar and rushed out of the palace. Down at the jousting ground a large crowd had

gathered. They were applauding Sir
Wilbert, who was lifting huge weights and
inviting people to feel his biceps.

Laura was standing at the edge of the
crowd.

"Laura!" puffed the Prince. "Is it true?
Have you really found a unicorn? However
did you do it?"

"I spoke to my friend Lucinda," said Laura
Jones. "She's got a pony called Buster. She
and Buster are in the Horse Show this
afternoon – they're in the Clowns' Parade."

"That's very interesting, Laura," said

Prince Pom. "But what's that to do with unicorns?"

"There's a Unicorn Class!" said Laura. "Lucinda says there's only one unicorn in the kingdom and it's owned by a girl called Elfrida. She wins the Unicorn Class every year because she's the only entrant."

"Bong!" The town clock struck midday.

"We can get there if we start now," said Laura Jones. "It's not far – just on the other side of Widgery Wood."

Behind them there was a storm of clapping. Sir Wilbert was doing press-ups.

"Come on, Titch!" he yelled, spotting the Prince. "Let's see how many you can do!"

"Let's go!" said Prince Pom.

The path through Widgery Wood was crowded with people on their way to the Horse Show.

Suddenly Prince Pom stopped and tugged at Laura's sleeve.

"Laura!" he whispered. "Over there!"

Laura looked where he was pointing, and she saw something white weaving its way through the trees.

"It's a unicorn, Laura!" cried Prince Pom.

"I'm sure it is. Come on!"

He took the salt cellar from his pocket and ran off into the wood.

"Your Highness!" called Laura as she ran after him. "I don't think that will work! The wizard was joking."

"Nonsense, Laura!" said the Prince. "The wizard never jokes."

Suddenly, just ahead of them, a unicorn appeared. It stood there, swishing its long golden tail, while the horn on its head sparkled in the sunlight. Prince Pom rushed at it, waving the salt cellar. In the blink of an eye, the unicorn was gone.

And so it went on. Every time the Prince got close, the animal sprang away and pranced deeper and deeper into the wood.

"I think we've lost it, Your Highness," said Laura at last.

"No!" cried Prince Pom. "There it is again!"

He started forward and then stopped as a girl danced out from behind an oak.

She wore a floaty white dress and there were flowers in her long golden hair. They

watched as she leaped and pirouetted over the patches of dappled sunlight and wove her way around the birches. At last she stopped, a little way off.

"Why were you chasing my unicorn?" she demanded.

Prince Pom gave a bow and the girl gave a curtsey. She was holding a bunch of wild flowers to her face.

"Elfrida, I presume," said the Prince politely. "We would like a hair from your unicorn's tail – if you can spare it."

"Oh!" said the girl. "I see." She thought for a moment. Then she said "Do you like dancing?"

"Er – er –" said Prince Pom, who didn't like dancing at all.

"I live for dancing!" said the girl, throwing her flowers in the air and dancing round a birch tree in a careless way. "It is my life.

35

That and my unicorn. Dance with me!"

"Go on, Your Highness," whispered Laura, nudging the Prince. "You did dancing at Finishing School, didn't you?"

"Er – what sort of dance would you like to do?" asked Prince Pom. "The waltz? Tango? Foxtrot?"

"Oh – none of those," said the girl, with a curl of her lip. "I am as free as the wind and I dance like the wind. This way! That way!" She swayed around. "Dance with

me and we'll see about the hair," she said.

There was nothing else for it. Prince Pom gave a huge sigh and followed Elfrida as she danced round trees and leaped over brambles. He hopped and skipped about, feeling extremely silly. His face was bright red and he was soon out of breath.

After what seemed ages the girl stopped.

"I think that's enough," she said. "I'll be late for the Horse Show."

She clicked her fingers and the unicorn came trotting towards them through the trees.

"What about the hair?" puffed the Prince.

Elfrida's manner changed abruptly.

"Clear off, you two oiks!" she said. "No-one touches my unicorn!"

"I am no oik," said Prince Pom, taken aback. "I am your Prince."

Elfrida clicked her fingers again and two enormous bodyguards stepped out from behind an oak.

"I don't care who you are!" she said. "You're a rubbish dancer. Be off before I set my men on you."

The bodyguards raised their cudgels and Prince Pom and Laura took to their heels.

"She tricked me!" panted the Prince as they reached the path. "What an awful girl!"

"Don't let's give up!" said Laura Jones. "Look! We're nearly at the Show Ground."

The Clowns' Parade was already in full swing.

"There's Lucinda!" said Laura and she waved at a girl in baggy red trousers, a big red nose and a gold, cone-shaped hat. She trotted along on a little white pony. Laura looked thoughtful.

"I've had an idea," she said. "Wait there, Your Highness. I won't be long."

Prince Pom waited. A little way off, under a tree, he could see Elfrida and her unicorn, with her armed ruffians standing guard on either side.

"This is hopeless," he thought miserably.

"I'm going to let my father down. And I'll be a laughing stock." Laura came back, looking pleased with herself, and at the same moment, Lucinda came riding out of the ring with the other clowns. Laura waved to her friend, who jumped off her pony.

A broad smile spread over Lucinda's face as Laura whispered in her ear.

"It might work, Laura!" she said. With that, she, Laura and the pony disappeared behind a horsebox.

"And now – the Unicorn Class!" called the announcer over the tannoy. "Ladies and Gentlemen – Elfrida Wildwood on her unicorn, Quicksilver!"

40

There was a spattering of applause and Elfrida ran into the middle of the ring, with the unicorn following her. She did a little dance while the unicorn pranced around behind her. Then she leaped upon its back.

"And we have a surprise new entrant this year!" called the announcer. "Please give a big hand for our very own Prince Pom on his unicorn, Buster!"

Prince Pom looked round wildly.

"Your Highness!"

The whisper came from behind him. He wheeled round and saw Laura and Lucinda

leading Buster towards him. They had fixed Lucinda's pointy hat to the pony's head by the elastic and arranged his mane around it so the join was hidden. Buster looked pleased with himself. He tossed his head and the flowers behind his ears quivered.

"Your unicorn, Your Highness," said Lucinda, and before the Prince had time to protest, she and Laura had hoisted him into the saddle.

"Take my scissors, Your Highness," said Laura. "Forget about the salt. Just try to get

as close as you can – then snip off a hair."

"Laura, I can't –" began Prince Pom, but it was too late. Lucinda gave Buster a smart tap and the next moment they were cantering into the ring, while the crowd whistled and stamped.

Elfrida was already in action. She balanced on the unicorn's back and stood on one leg. Then she waved her arms about in a dreamy sort of way.

Prince Pom thought he'd better trot after her, but however fast he went, Elfrida went faster. She was much too quick for him.

"Idiot!" she hissed as she flashed past. She wheeled round and started to circle him. Prince Pom noticed that she was standing on her head. Then she did a back flip. The Prince was so surprised that he dropped the scissors.

"Unicorn-riding is an art-form," hissed Elfrida, as she whirled past him, lying along the unicorn's back. "You look like a sack of potatoes."

"Unicorns! Approach the judging stand!" cried the announcer.

"You haven't got a chance!" sneered Elfrida, deliberately bumping the unicorn into Buster's side. "You're pathetic."

Her unicorn curled its lip and made a sniggering sound.

It was that snigger that did it. It was just too much for Buster. He bared his teeth and whinneyed with rage. Then he reached forward and nipped the unicorn's bottom.

"Help!" screamed Elfrida as the unicorn

reared up in surprise. "Help!" Elfrida screamed again as it began to career round and round the ring, with Buster in hot pursuit.

It was over almost before it had started. The unicorn swerved off to the left and leaped a hedge. Then it galloped away into the wood and Elfrida's screams of rage faded into the distance.

"So, Laura," said Prince Pom later that day, as they walked back to town. "Your plan didn't work and I am going to be pulverized by Sir Wilbert."

"That's what you think, Your Highness," said Laura Jones and she pulled up her sleeve. There was something coiled around her wrist — something that glittered in the sunshine.

"Laura!" said the Prince in a trembling voice. "Is that —"

"Yes!" said Laura. "It's a unicorn's hair. When I went to get my scissors back I had a look at the hedge — you know, the one the unicorn jumped. And I found this — all tangled up in the twigs."

"Hooray!" cried Prince Pom. "Laura — you're a star!"

"And *you* won first prize in the Unicorn Class," said Laura, nodding at the giant cream cake the Prince was carrying. "I think it's been a very successful day, don't you?"

"Oh yes!" cried the Prince. "It looks as though my luck's beginning to change!"

He spoke too soon, however. As they passed Sir Wilbert's door, the Knight poked his head out.

"I'll have that!" he said and snatched the cake.

"He's so greedy!" said Prince Pom. "Oh – never mind. Let him have it."

They continued on to the wizard's room, where the Prince knocked and called out, "We've got it!"

The wizard opened the door. He looked surprised.

"And now I suppose you'll be wanting to drop this into your cauldron," said the Prince, holding out the coil of golden hair.

The wizard chuckled.

"Not at all," he said. "It's not going to be boiled. It's going to be knitted."

"What?" cried the Prince.

The wizard held out a crumpled piece of paper, covered with coffee stains.

"Here's the pattern," he said. "You must knit the unicorn's hair into a pullover. With all the other threads. It will protect you in battle and give you the Strength of Ten."

"Knit it?" said the Prince in dismay. "But I don't know how to knit. Laura – could you do it for me?"

"No she can't!" snapped the wizard. "Only the wearer may knit it. Otherwise it won't work."

And with that, he turned on his heel and slammed the door.

The Beast of Beltrane

Prince Pom got up early the next morning. He thought of asking his mother for advice, but she was busy fussing around his father's leg, so he just borrowed two needles from her knitting bag instead.

"It shouldn't be too difficult," he thought. But it was. The unicorn hair was slippery and he couldn't get it to stay on the needles.

In the end he sent a message to Laura Jones.

"I can't do it, Laura!" he said when she poked her head round the door. "It's too hard."

"I've had an idea, Your Highness," said Laura Jones and she reached into her rucksack. She pulled out a long strip of

lumpy-looking material, with two needles sticking out of it.

"What's that?" asked Prince Pom.

"It's a scarf," said Laura. "I've been knitting it since I was five. I thought that if I knitted, you could watch what I do and follow me."

So they started, and after a while Prince Pom had a whole row of knitting on his needles. Then another. And another.

"Oh, Laura!" sighed the Prince as he finished row four. "Do you think this is going to work? I don't even know if the wizard's got the spell right."

"Let's have a break," suggested Laura. "We could have a think about the next part of the spell."

"But I've never even heard of the Beast of Beltrane until now," said Prince Pom. "However do we find it?"

"We could ask the Royal Librarian," said Laura Jones.

"The Beast of Beltrane?" said the librarian, looking at them over his spectacles. "Let's see ..."

He tottered to the top of a step ladder and took down a heavy book.

"Aha! Here we are!" he said, thumbing through its dusty pages. "'The Beast of Beltrane: the Leader of the Wild Hunt. He leads his pack through the forests on moonlit nights, hunting down his prey.'"

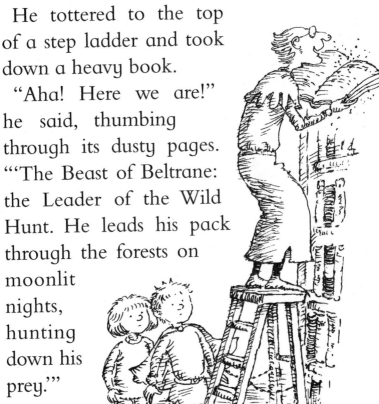

"What's he hunting?" asked Prince Pom.

"No-one knows," said the librarian, closing the book. "It's a mystery. Rabbits? Dreams? Children? You know he's coming when you hear a wild howling. Then all you can do is run."

"Laura," said Prince Pom, who thought it all sounded too scary for words. "However are we going to get this terrible Beast's whiskers?"

"Let me think about it," said Laura. "But before I forget – I have something for Sir Wilbert. Will you come with me?"

They found Sir Wilbert leaning against a pillar. He was reading a newspaper. The rabbit sat at his feet, looking depressed.

"See you've won a unicorn race, Titch!" he said, waving the sports page at them. "Ha! Ha! That will help you in the joust. I *don't* think! Ha! Ha! Ha!"

Laura curtseyed and reached into her rucksack.

"A present, sire!" she said.

"Yummy! Chocolate eclairs!" said Sir Wilbert. He grabbed the cakes and disappeared into his room. The rabbit hopped after him.

"I don't know why you're giving him cakes, Laura," complained Prince Pom. "You should have seen what he ate at dinner last night – at least half an ox. And then he kept everyone up late singing rude songs."

Laura just smiled.

"Could you meet me at the edge of the wood at six, Your Highness?" she said. "And bring some workmen with spades. I've just had a brainwave."

Prince Pom borrowed some money from the Head Cook and hired four workmen. They grumbled as they followed him and Laura deep into the wood.

"I don't usually work for peanuts," said one.

"It's daylight robbery!" said another.

Prince Pom pretended not to hear.

"This is a good spot," said Laura, stopping suddenly. "Do you think you could dig a hole here, right across the path?"

The workmen went on grumbling, but they set to work. They dug deeper and deeper until they disappeared from view.

Prince Pom watched the flying spadefuls of earth and whistled to himself. Laura was already collecting leaves and branches to disguise the trap.

"I should stop that, sire, if I was you," said one of the workmen, popping his head out of the hole. "The Beast of Beltrane eats whistlers. It is well-known."

Dusk was falling. The moon slid from behind a cloud and a wild howling shattered the stillness.

"We're off!" said the workmen, and they flung down their spades, clambered out of the pit and ran away. The howl rang out again.

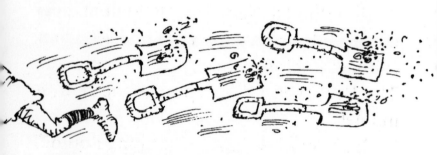

"Er – perhaps we should go, too," said Prince Pom, but Laura Jones took no notice of him.

"Come on, Your Highness!" she said. "Help me with these branches!"

When they had covered the pit, Laura stepped back and dusted her hands.

"Now," she said. "I'm going to hide behind

this tree. I have a net in my rucksack."

"And me, Laura?" said the Prince. He was beginning to feel suspicious. "What do you want me to do?"

"Oh – nothing much," said Laura. "Just stand over there. And whistle."

"You must be joking!" said Prince Pom. The howling seemed closer now. "I'm not doing that!"

"It will be all right, Your Highness," said Laura. "When you see the Wild Hunt coming, just run. Then jump over the pit. The Beast will fall in and I'll trap him in my net."

"Can't you do the whistling, Laura?" asked the Prince.

"Not really," said Laura. "You're much better at it than me."

Prince Pom walked a little way down the path.

"What shall I whistle?" he whispered over his shoulder.

"Anything you like, Your Highness," said Laura Jones.

So Prince Pom whistled 'The Teddy Bears' Picnic' and all the while the howls of the Wild Hunt drew closer and closer.

"Keep whistling!" hissed Laura.

Then, with a rushing, pounding noise, the Wild Hunt was upon them. Red eyes glowed in the shadows and down the path thundered a mass of dark shapes. Prince Pom was frozen to the spot.

"Run, Your Highness!" called Laura.

With a mighty effort, Prince Pom turned and ran, and just at that moment, the moon

disappeared behind a cloud. In a panic, the
Prince gave a leap and – Crash! – he felt
himself falling through branches and leaves.
He was dimly aware of something falling
in beside him while the rest of the Hunt
streamed over his head. Then all was silent.

Laura appeared above him.

"You mis-timed your jump a little, Your
Highness!" she said.

"Help!" screamed the Prince. "Laura – it's
down here with me!"

Laura shone her torch until its beam picked out a small wallaby. It hopped up and down, looking cross.

"I suppose that must be the Beast," said Laura. She held out her scissors. "Here, Your Highness. Could you snip off a couple of whiskers?"

Prince Pom reached up and took the scissors and Laura shone the torch. The Prince gave a wail.

"Laura!" he cried. "It's no good! Oh woe! The Beast has no whiskers!"

The wallaby blinked in the torchlight and Laura saw that the Prince was right; it had no whiskers at all.

"Hang on!" she said. "Perhaps that's not the Beast. Listen!'

A howl came echoing down the path. And then another.

"It's coming round again!" said Laura and nipped behind her tree.

"Don't leave me!" cried Prince Pom.

Something came blundering through the dark. There was a howl and a crash and whatever it was landed next to the Prince and the wallaby. Laura stepped forward and threw the net.

"Help! Help!" screamed Prince Pom, lashing around in its folds, but this time his cries were mixed with a mournful howling.

The moon came out from behind the cloud and Laura could see a large dark shape writhing under the net.

"Get me out!" screamed Prince Pom, and to Laura's surprise, another voice joined in.

"Help!" it shouted. "Get me out too!"

It was an old man with a bald head and a long moustache. Prince Pom wriggled around until he was free. He cut the net away from the old man with Laura's scissors and then, with a lot of pushing and pulling, they got him out of the pit. The Prince lifted the wallaby up and scrambled out himself. Then he and Laura stared at the old man.

He was a strange sight. He wore shorts and running shoes and his knees were covered in cuts and bruises. His moustache was so long that it trailed behind him on the ground.

"What were you doing to my Lulu?" the old man demanded, stroking the wallaby.

"We just wanted two of her whiskers," said Prince Pom.

The old man looked puzzled.

"Are you part of the Wild Hunt?" asked Laura.

"Yes," said the old man, starting to walk away. He tripped over his moustache and fell down. He gave a low wail, picked himself up and started off again, with the wallaby hopping along behind.

"But where is the Beast of Beltrane?" called Prince Pom.

The old man stopped dead in his tracks. He drew himself to his full height.

"Here!" he said. "Look no further! *I* am the Beast of Beltrane!"

There was a startled silence. At last Prince Pom said:

"You? The Beast of Beltrane? Pray explain yourself, sir."

The old man sank down on a log and the wallaby nuzzled up to him.

"Wait!" said Laura. "Let's have a look at those knees."

She took a small first aid kit from her rucksack and cleaned the old man's wounds. Then she put sticking-plasters on them.

"Thank you!" said the old man. He rose to his feet and attempted to bow, but tripped over his moustache again. Laura helped him up.

"I am the last of the Beasts!" he said. "The Beast family, of Castle Beltrane. I am the Leader of the Wild Hunt."

"But what are you hunting?" asked Laura.

"Oh – nothing!" said the old man. "My family hunted, back in the bad old days. But I don't go in for it at all – quite the opposite. I run an animal sanctuary. I love animals."

"What sort of animals?" asked Prince Pom suspiciously.

"Oh, little woodland creatures!" said the old man. "You know – foxes! Badgers! Deer! And the odd animal like Lulu here," he said, patting the wallaby, "who have escaped from zoos."

"So why are you running around in the woods?" asked Laura.

"Exercise!" said the old man. "We always race on moonlit nights. We see how fast we can get round the course."

"And the howling?" asked Laura.

"Oh – that was me, I'm afraid," said the old man. "I'm meant to be leader but I always come last. I keep tripping over my moustache."

"Then why don't you cut it?" asked Prince Pom.

"Impossible!" said the Beast. "I have no

scissors. Sharp instruments are banned in Castle Beltrane."

"I could cut it for you if you like," said Laura Jones.

"Oh – would you?" cried the old man.

So Laura took her scissors from Prince Pom and trimmed the Beast's moustache. She even curled the ends for him. The Beast admired himself in her mirror.

"Oh – thank you!" he cried. "That's really smart."

"Would you mind if we took a couple of whiskers?" asked Laura.

"Not at all!" said the Beast. "And I'll take

the rest for my wrens. They can line their nests with it."

Then he raced off down the path and Lulu bounded after him.

Laura and the Prince walked back to town in the moonlight. The Prince looped the whiskers round his hands and Laura

wound them into a ball. In the distance they could hear someone strumming a banjo and singing at the top of his voice.

"That will be Sir Wilbert," said Prince

Pom. "Singing to the ladies-in-waiting."

"He's got a horrible voice, hasn't he?" said Laura. They had reached her house. "Good night, Your Highness. And good luck with the knitting."

The Secret of the Labyrinth

The King of Little Twittelberg hopped into the breakfast room on his crutches and collapsed into a chair.

"It is time for the Taunting!" he said. "Let the Taunting begin!"

Prince Pom knew what was expected of him. He looked across the table at Sir Wilbert, who was tucking into a huge plate of bacon and eggs and dangling a lettuce leaf in front of the rabbit.

"Sire! I challenge you to mortal combat!" he said in a wobbly voice.

"I accept!" said Sir Wilbert, through a mouthful of bacon. "Let the best man win. That's me," he added, jerking the lettuce

leaf away as the rabbit made a lunge for it.

"I am a fearless fighter!" said Prince Pom. (He had heard his father say this in the past.)

Sir Wilbert roared with laughter and flexed his biceps.

"I have never lost a fight!" he thundered. "I have defeated a thousand men in single-handed combat!"

Prince Pom lost his nerve.

"Fishface!" he said.

"Skinnyribs!" retorted Sir Wilbert.

And so it went on, until at last the King cried "Halt! That's enough Taunting for today."

He looked at his son.

"What's that you've got there, Pom?" he asked as the Prince tried to hide something under the table. "No, no. Hold it up."

Slowly, and blushing scarlet, Prince Pom

held up his knitting. There was a stunned silence and then Sir Wilbert let out a great roar of laughter.

"Really, Pom!" said the King. "I'm

pleased you've taken up a hobby — but at a time like this? Surely you should be practising your jousting?"

Sir Wilbert gave another roar of laughter.

"It calms my nerves, father," stuttered Prince Pom, who could think of nothing else to say.

The King snorted.

"Well, *I* like knitting," said the Queen. "He must get it from me."

"It was so embarrassing, Laura," said the Prince when they met up later that morning in the Town Square. "I could have sunk through the floor."

"Never mind, Your Highness!" said Laura Jones. "Look! We're in luck!"

ALL ABOARD FOR THE LABYRINTH! FUN! EXCITEMENT! FAIRY GROTTOS!

She pointed to where a coach was waiting. Next to it was a poster that said 'All aboard for the Labyrinth! Fun! Excitement! Fairy Grottos!'

The coach was already packed with tourists, so Laura and the Prince sat outside, next to the coachman. He clicked his tongue at the horses and the coach rattled away over the cobbles and into the countryside.

After a while they turned down a dusty lane. In the distance a clump of jagged white rocks rose above the surrounding fields.

"There's the labyrinth!" said the coachman. "Giddy-up, girls!"

They drew nearer and they saw a little hut with a sign saying 'Ticket Office'. An old lady peered out. She looked pleased to see them.

"My first visitors this week!" she said. "Tickets are one groat each. Would you like a free map?"

She handed everyone a map of the labyrinth. It looked very complicated. It had little signs all over it – 'Fairy Grotto', 'Troll Bridge' and 'Crocodile Pool'.

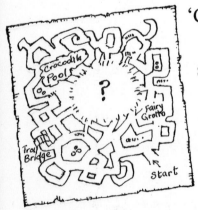

"What's this white space in the middle?" asked Prince Pom.

"Oh, no-one's ever reached the middle," said the old lady.

"Including me. It's a mystery. If you do get there, there's a prize. Good luck."

Laura noticed that their fellow tourists were not looking at their maps. They were all staring at Prince Pom.

"A real live Prince!" said a tubby man in bermuda shorts. "Say, Your Highness, would you mind posing with our Elmer?"

"Oh – not at all," said the Prince, who was always polite, and he put his arm round the little boy's shoulders while his father took a photo.

And that was only the start of it. The other tourists crowded round, taking photos, staring and asking the Prince for autographs.

"Your Highness!" said Laura, plucking at the Prince's sleeve. "Perhaps we should make a start?"

The old lady had worked very hard to make the labyrinth attractive to visitors. There were little plastic animals in crannies in the rocks and plaster gnomes standing by pools.

"Oh look! There's the Fairy Grotto!" said Laura, pointing at a group of fairies having a tea party.

"Huh!" grunted the Prince.

The tourists padded along behind them. They took no notice of the Fairy Grotto; they were too busy staring at the Prince.

"Are we near the middle yet, Laura?" asked Prince Pom, who was beginning to tire of the attention.

"I'm not sure," said Laura. "I don't think it's a very good map. Look! There's that crocodile again."

"And haven't we been over Troll Bridge once already?" asked the Prince.

"The Prince says we've been over Troll Bridge already!" echoed the tourists.

"Let's try this passageway here," said Laura. "It doesn't seem to be marked on the map."

They made their way along a winding track. The sun shone on the white walls

above them and every so often a bird burst into song. The tourists trotted happily along behind them.

"I wish they'd go away!" whispered Prince Pom, but Laura wasn't listening. She was staring at a strand of red wool that wound its way along the side of the path.

"This must be it!" she said.

They followed the wool and the tourists followed them. Everything had gone quiet. Even the birds had stopped singing.

"HUUR-UMPH!"

The silence was shattered by a rumbling noise that came rolling down the passageway towards them. It rumbled

away into the distance like thunder and then all was still again.

"What was that?" whispered Prince Pom.

"I don't know," said Laura Jones. "Let's find out."

They started to hurry. Prince Pom was

hoping to shake off the tourists but they stuck close to his heels. In front of him, Laura held up her hand and stopped. The Prince bumped into her and everyone else bumped into him.

They were standing at the entrance to a huge arena, in the middle of which was a chalk pillar. And tied around this pillar was the end of the red wool.

"Hurray!" cried Prince Pom and he darted forwards. Everyone else ran after him.

The rumble sounded again. The noise seemed to be coming from a cave to their right. Then it changed into a snorting, spluttering sound, like someone waking from a deep sleep. There was an earth-shattering roar and a terrifying figure leaped out into the sunshine.

"Oh dear!" said Laura Jones. "I think it's a minotaur!"

The monster advanced towards them, swishing its tail. It was enormous. It had the head and chest of a buffalo and its hairy legs were clad in baggy blue boxer shorts.

"Fight!" it roared, lowering its head. "Fight!"

The tourists applauded and settled themselves on ledges around the side of the arena. They started unpacking sandwiches and bottles of lemonade.

"Fight!" roared the monster again and it jumped in front of the passageway so that the escape route was blocked.

Laura thought quickly. She noticed a little boy nearby tucking into a bag of marshmallows.

"I think the Prince would like to borrow those," she said. "Do you mind?"

The little boy frowned and hid the bag behind his back but his mother grabbed it and handed it to Laura.

"It's for the Prince, Eric," she said.

Laura rolled a marshmallow at the minotaur, who stopped roaring and gobbled it up. The tourists clapped.

"Keep it occupied, Your Highness!" she said, thrusting a handful of marshmallows at the Prince. "I'll grab the wool and start making my way back. When the coast's clear, just run for it."

"But how will I find my way out?" quavered the Prince.

"I'll leave a trail," said Laura Jones.

The minotaur danced around the Prince, its hooves raised like a boxer's fists. The Prince rolled a marshmallow and the monster stopped dancing and wolfed it down.

"More!"
it roared. So
the Prince did
it again. And again. Out of
the corner of his eye he could see Laura
untying the wool and backing towards
the entrance. The tourists sat there and
munched away at their sandwiches. They
looked as though they were enjoying
themselves.

"WAAAH!" roared the monster and
charged.

"Oh no!" thought the Prince. "I've run
out of marshmallows!"

There was nothing else for it. He made a

dash for the chalk pillar and the monster charged after him. Round and round they went. Every so often the minotaur skidded to a halt and changed direction and the Prince had to be quick on his feet to avoid being caught.

"Hurray for the Prince!" cried the tourists, and they gave a Mexican Wave.

"I can't keep this up for much longer!" thought Prince Pom. "What would Laura do? Oh – I know!"

He ran out into the arena and held up his

cloak. The minotaur snorted and pawed the ground. Then it charged. At the last moment Prince Pom whipped his cloak away and the monster thundered past him.

The tourists gave another Mexican Wave. The Prince ran back to the middle of the arena. He held up his cloak again and flapped it at the minotaur.

The tourists cheered.

Then the monster was thundering towards him and once more the Prince neatly side-stepped. Crash! The minotaur collided with the pillar and fell flat on its face. There was a moment's silence and then it started to snore.

The crowd broke into wild applause.

Prince Pom bowed and the tourists snapped away on their cameras. Then the Prince made a bolt for the passageway. Everyone stampeded after him and behind them the snores of the minotaur echoed round the empty arena.

"She said she'd leave a trail!" thought Prince Pom. "Where is it? Where is it?"

"Look!" cried a little boy. "A marshmallow!"

And, sure enough, there was a white marshmallow, lying at the entrance to a side turning. The Prince swerved and the tourists did

the same. The Prince saw another white marshmallow, then a pink one. At last, as he rounded a corner, he saw Laura Jones. She was holding a ball of red wool.

"Hallo, Your Highness," said Laura. "How did it go? Was it difficult?"

"Well, yes —" began the Prince, but Laura interrupted him.

"We're on the right path!" she said. "There's Troll Bridge!"

The old lady leaned out of the ticket office when she saw them coming towards her.

"Did you find the middle?" she asked.

"Yes!" puffed the Prince.

"Well done!" she said. "Here's your prize!"

It was a red-nosed gnome, holding a fishing rod.

"Fantastic show, madam!" said one of the tourists. "The Prince was spectacular!"

"But did you like the Fairy Grotto?" asked the old lady, looking puzzled.

They could still hear her shouting as the coach rattled away down the track.

"Tell all your friends!" she was yelling. "Tell them to come to the labyrinth and see the Fairy Grotto!"

The tourists were still chattering away about the Prince when the coach trundled into the Town Square. Laura and Prince Pom sneaked away.

When they reached Laura's house she

darted inside and came out holding a huge cake.

"Could you give this to Sir Wilbert for me, Your Highness?" she asked.

"A chocolate gateau?" said Prince Pom. "I don't think Sir Wilbert deserves a chocolate gateau. I deserve it more than he does, Laura. Why are you giving him all these cakes?"

Laura just smiled and the Prince turned away, feeling puzzled. But Laura called him back.

"Aren't you forgetting something, Your Highness?" she asked.

And she handed him the ball of red wool.

The Griffin

Days passed and Prince Pom stayed in his room and knitted. There was not much time left and he was worried.

"Hallo, Your Highness!" said Laura Jones, popping her head round the door. "I've got good news."

"Oh, has Sir Wilbert given up and gone home?" asked Prince Pom. "Knit one – purl one –"

"No," said Laura. "He hasn't. But I know

where we can find a griffin."

"Oh, good," said Prince Pom, who still hadn't got to the end of the red wool.

"Yes!" said Laura. "It turns out that my Uncle Charlie is a griffin-spotter."

"A what?" said the Prince.

"A griffin-spotter," repeated Laura. "And he's going to the Griffin Reserve today with some other spotters. He says we can have a ride there in their wagon. And he says to bring some binoculars."

As Prince Pom and Laura hurried across the Great Hall, they came across Sir Wilbert, who was throwing carrots for the rabbit to fetch.

"Hallo, Loser!" roared the Knight and he strolled over and stood on Prince Pom's toe. "Little squirt!" he said.

"It's all right, Laura," said Prince Pom. "It's just the Taunting. It's the custom. Vile poltroon!" he squeaked.

"What's it to be, then?" rumbled the Knight. "Knitting needles at dawn?"

Prince Pom winced. He wished Sir Wilbert would get off his toe.

"I've brought you a present, Sire," said Laura Jones and she reached into her rucksack.

"Not Lemon Drizzle cake?" cried the Knight and he jumped off the Prince's toe and snatched it from her. "Yummy!"

Prince Pom and Laura turned and ran.

The griffin-spotters sang songs and swapped griffin stories all the way to the griffin reserve. The wagon lurched along, only stopping when it reached a rock-strewn clearing in the trees.

The spotters piled out and made a bee-line for a little hut on legs.

"This is the best place to spot griffins," said Laura's uncle as they climbed the ladder.

"Where do they nest, Uncle Charlie?" asked Laura.

"Who knows?" said her uncle. "We've never seen a nest — or an egg or a young griffin, come to that. All we do know is that griffins love gold. We usually leave a coin or two out on that rock."

Laura and the Prince peered through one of the little windows and saw a griffin-spotter hurrying back to the hut, holding a purse.

"Quick, Bill!" Uncle Charlie yelled. "There's one coming now!"

The spotter fell into the hut and the others crowded to the windows. Laura and the Prince just had time to see a monstrous shape, half eagle, half lion, come swooping from the sky and then they were pushed to one side by the press of griffin-spotters.

"This is no good!" whispered Laura. "We need a closer look – we have to follow one to its nest."

They slid down the steps. The Prince lifted his gold binoculars to his eyes and the sunlight glinted on his crown.

"I can't see a thing!" he said.

"Laura – there's another thing about griffins!" shouted Uncle Charlie from the hide as a dark shadow blotted out the sun. "I forgot –"

Too late! The next moment Laura and the Prince felt themselves seized in a pair of sharp talons.

"I forgot to tell you!" Uncle Charlie's voice, far below them, drifted over the tree-tops. "They eat people!"

The griffin carried them over the forest and circled round a tall pine. Then it dropped them.

"Help!" screamed Prince Pom.

But he need not have worried. They only fell a few feet and landed on something soft.

"We've found a griffin's nest!" whispered Laura.

The nest was beautiful. It glittered and shone with stolen treasures. Golden coins, watches and goblets were scattered about and the sides were lined with woven strands of gold. In the middle of the nest was a big blue egg.

With a loud squawk, the griffin dropped out of the sky. It sat facing them with a nasty look on its face. Suddenly it clacked its beak, leaned forward and seized Prince Pom's crown. It clacked its beak again and swished its tail.

"Do you think it's going to eat us?" whispered the Prince, shifting uneasily; he was sitting on a gold necklace.

"I hope not," said Laura. "Quick – hand me your binoculars."

The griffin opened its beak wide and stretched forward. Then it stopped. Laura was swinging the binoculars from side to side. The sun sparkled on them and the griffin's head began to move from side to side too, as it followed the glinting arc. The nest swayed gently in the breeze and the only sound was a soft tapping that seemed to be coming from the egg.

"You are sleepy!" murmured Laura. "Very, very sleepy."

The griffin's heavy eyelids began to close. Suddenly it fell back and started snoring.

"Quick! Let's get out of here!" said the Prince.

"A good idea!" said Laura Jones. "But first – help me unwind these gold threads."

Carefully, very carefully, so as not to wake the sleeping griffin, they began to untangle the gold strands from the inside of the nest. The griffin snored and the tapping from the egg grew louder.

"That's three!" said Laura and she looped the gold strands round her neck.

"Crack!"

The sound came from the egg. To their amazement splits began to appear all over it and then the blue shell fell apart. And there, in the middle, sat a baby griffin. It was staring straight at Prince Pom. It gave a squeak. Then it jumped onto his shoulder

and started nuzzling his ear.

"It thinks you're its mother," said Laura. "Put it down, Your Highness. We've got to go."

She was already lowering herself over the edge of the nest. The Prince grabbed his crown and followed her and the baby griffin began to squeak in distress.

Ages seemed to pass before they reached the forest floor. They dropped the last few feet and landed with a thump on a bed of pine needles.

"We'd better run for it," said Laura.

But at that moment there was a loud squealing and something came bouncing down through the branches and landed at their feet. It was the baby griffin. It looked up at Prince Pom and squeaked.

"Let's go!" said Prince Pom.

They started to run and the baby griffin ran after them. It bounded along on its little legs, tripping over tussocks and bumping into rocks.

"Run faster!" panted Laura.

"I think we've shaken it off!" gasped the Prince as the cries of the baby griffin died away into the distance.

They sank down onto a log to catch their breath. Prince Pom was just admiring the gold strands and wondering whether they'd be easy to knit, when they heard a squeaking sound, and round a bend in the track came the baby griffin. It rushed at Prince Pom and leaped onto his knee. It sat there, gazing up at him.

"Let's go, Your Highness!" said Laura.

Prince Pom placed the baby griffin firmly on the path and said "Stay!" in a stern voice, but the baby wouldn't be put off and bounced

along
behind
 them as
  they ran.

At last, just when they felt they could run no further, they burst into the clearing. The griffin-spotters came tumbling down the stairs of the little hut and ran towards them. To Prince Pom's surprise they ran straight past him and Laura and made a circle round the baby griffin.

"Glad to see you're safe, Laura!" cried Uncle Charlie. "And you've brought us a baby griffin! However did you do it?"

Laura had no time to reply, because the baby griffin set up a terrible squealing and started hopping up and down.

"It wants the Prince," said Laura.

So the spotters cleared a path and the baby griffin rushed at Prince Pom, who

was resting on a rock. It leaped onto his knee and peered up at him. The spotters crowded round once more, jostling each other, taking notes and snapping away on their cameras.

"Would you mind moving to one side, Your Highness?" they said. "We'd like one of the baby griffin on its own."

The Prince moved away and left the baby on the rock. To his surprise it didn't protest. It was looking at the cameras. It seemed fascinated. It twirled round. It lifted one leg in the air. Then the other.

Then it turned a
somersault and
stood on its head.
The griffin-spotters
were enchanted and
snapped away to their hearts' content. And
the more they exclaimed, the more the
baby griffin loved it.

It began doing cartwheels.

The spotters were so
engrossed that only Laura
Jones noticed the squawking
sounds in the distance.

"Its mother's coming!" she cried.

Everyone began to race towards the hut.
The baby griffin hopped along after them.

"Not so fast!" said Laura and she grabbed it and set it down on the rock.

"Eeeek! Eeeek!" screamed the baby griffin.

"What are we going to do, Laura?" cried Prince Pom, in a panic. The squawks of the mother griffin were getting closer all the time.

In answer, Laura reached into her rucksack and brought out her mirror. She propped it up on the rock and placed the

baby griffin in front of it. The baby stopped squealing and started to pose, twisting and turning and admiring its reflection in the shiny glass.

Laura and the Prince ran for it. Not a moment too soon!

The mother griffin came swooping from the sky, scooped up its baby and flapped away over the tree-tops.

The griffin-spotters were over the moon. They chattered all the way home.

"It's the first baby griffin ever sighted in Little Twittelberg!" cried Uncle Charlie.

Laura fingered the loops of golden thread around her neck.

"And I've brought something else back," she whispered to Prince Pom.

She reached into her pocket. Prince Pom stared.

"Are those what I think they are, Laura?" he said.

Back at the palace they went straight to the wizard's room and knocked at his door.

"What is it?" came the wizard's voice.

"We've got something for you!" called Prince Pom.

"What?" said the wizard, peering out.

"Look what we found in a griffin's nest!" said Laura. "It must have snatched them from your windowsill."

"My spectacles! My magic spectacles!" cried the wizard and grabbed them from her.

"And now you have them again," said Prince Pom to the wizard's disappearing back, "we wondered if you'd check my spell and make sure you got it right."

The wizard grumbled away to himself and disappeared into his room. He was back in a flash with the spectacles perched on his nose.

"The spell is correct!" he said.

"Oh, good!" said Prince Pom.

"Almost correct!" said the wizard.

"What do you mean, 'almost correct'?" asked Prince Pom.

"What I said!" snapped the wizard. "I got a few minor details wrong but that shouldn't matter. Now buzz off."

"Really, Laura!" said Prince Pom as the door slammed in their faces. "I think he must be the rudest wizard ever!"

The Magic Pullover

The day of the tournament dawned bright and clear. A huge crowd gathered by the jousting ground.

"Hurray!" they cried as Sir Wilbert swaggered across the field from his tent. Prince Pom walked to meet him. They bowed to each other.

"You've had it, Shorty!" growled Sir Wilbert, then he turned and swaggered back the way he had come.

"They go to their tents now and dress in their armour," said the King, idly flicking through a newspaper. 'Baby Griffin Spotted!' read the headline.

The Queen pointed at Prince Pom, who was sprinting down the field.

"My brave son!" she said. "He's in a hurry to start!"

Prince Pom tore back into his tent, where he found Laura Jones waiting for him. He took up his needles and started knitting for all he was worth.

"I've almost finished!" he said. "I've been up all night, Laura. All I've got to do now is sew the sides together."

Laura peeped round the tent-flap. At the far side of the field she could see Sir Wilbert's black and red tent, with his horse pawing the ground outside.

"YAAAH!"

An angry roar made everyone jump.

"What was that?" said Prince Pom. "Oh – I suppose it's just Sir Wilbert trying to scare me. Look, Laura! It's done!"

"That's very good, Your Highness," said Laura as the Prince held up the finished knitting.

The pullover was rather lumpy-looking. It was a mixture of red, silver and gold and there were a few holes where the Prince had dropped stitches. Prince Pom bit his lip.

"Do you think it's cheating, Laura?" he asked.

Laura had no time to answer.

"YAAAH!" Another roar came from Sir Wilbert's tent. A flock of starlings took flight and the waiting horse jumped and skittered about. And out of the tent shot Sir Wilbert's mascot, its eyes wide with terror. It raced down the field, making a beeline for the Prince's tent.

Prince Pom was still holding his knitting and saying, "I don't know if I should —" when the rabbit streaked through the tent flap, gave a bound and leaped straight at him. The Prince let go of the pullover and the rabbit rolled over and over on the floor, caught in a tangle of red, silver and gold.

Sir Wilbert rushed out of his tent, wearing only his underclothes. He gave a roar of rage and started to dance around on the spot. Prince Pom and Laura forgot all about the rabbit.

"YAAAH!" they heard Sir Wilbert

yell. "Someone's shrunk my armour! I've been bewitched!"

A moment or two passed before Laura and the Prince turned back to the rabbit. When they did, they both gasped. The mascot was growing. It grew bigger and

bigger until at last the pullover split and fell to the floor. But still the rabbit went on growing. It towered above them.

"Laura – the spell worked!" cried Prince Pom, stepping back. "Well, almost!"

His voice seemed to startle the rabbit. It gave a huge leap and uprooted the tent.

Then it bounded down the field towards Sir Wilbert. Laura and the Prince were left standing in the open.

The crowd supposed it must be part of the entertainment, and burst into wild

applause. Sir Wilbert stood rooted to the spot as the tent came hopping towards him. The rabbit turned a somersault and shook itself free. The crowd applauded even more loudly.

When it reached Sir Wilbert, the rabbit stopped. It turned and caught the Knight a wallop with its back feet.

"Ooh!" gasped the crowd as Sir Wilbert

sailed through the air. "Ah!" they cried as he landed on his back.

Sir Wilbert sat up. The rabbit was dancing round him, making threatening gestures. The Knight moved quickly for so large a man. He ran to his horse, vaulted onto its back and galloped away.

The rabbit watched him go. Then it dusted down its paws and lolloped away into the wood. The crowd went mad.

The King summoned Prince Pom to the royal podium.

"Where did that rabbit come from, my son?" he asked.

"I don't really know, father," said Prince Pom. "It just appeared."

"Ah well, the forests of Little Twittelberg abound with strange beasts," said the King. "Only yesterday, I believe, a baby griffin was spotted in our woods."

"Really, father?" said Prince Pom.

The King reached under his seat and brought out a rosette. He pinned it to the Prince's chest.

"You are a credit to me, my boy!" he said.

"You were ready to stand up to Sir Wilbert. He's run away, so it's a walkover. I declare you the winner."

The crowd cheered as the Queen presented the Prince with a purse containing four golden guineas.

"And now, my son," said the King, as he held out a pen. "You may sign my plaster. It's coming off tomorrow."

The next day Prince Pom scooted down to the playground on his new rollerblades.

He found Laura Jones on a swing.

"Here, Laura," he said. "I'd like to share my prize with you."

"Thank you, Your Highness," said Laura, taking the two gold coins. "I'll put them in my piggy-bank."

Prince Pom spun round on his blades.

"So the spell did work – in a way," he said. "I don't think I would have wanted to grow that big, though. I just wanted to be strong."

He thought for a while.

"I wonder who shrank Sir Wilbert's

armour?" he said at last. "Do you think someone put a spell on him?"

Laura giggled.

"It wasn't magic — it was my Plan B!" she said. "The armour didn't shrink — Sir Wilbert just grew too big for it!"

Prince Pom's eyes widened.

"It was all those cakes!" he said. "Laura Jones — you're a genius!"

A cloud passed over his face.

"What an awful fortnight!" he said. "I'm glad it's over! I've landed in a pit with the Beast of Beltrane, been chased by a minotaur and carried off by a griffin. And do you know what the very worst thing of all was, Laura?"

"No, Your Highness?" said Laura Jones.

"It was having to dance with that ghastly Elfrida Wildwood," said the Prince. "Ugh! I won't forget that in a hurry."

Laura had jumped off the swing and was climbing the steps of the slide.

"And now," said Prince Pom, looking up

at her. "I find I didn't have to do any of those things after all."

"Look on the bright side, Your Highness," said Laura. "You won the joust! And you've got your rollerblades. And you've learned

something new," she added as she came whizzing down the slide.

"What's that, Laura?" asked Prince Pom. Laura landed at his feet with a thump. "You've learned how to knit!" she said.